Mia's Mission
to be a
Mathematician!

LISA GOODSON

ISBN 978-1-64300-581-2 (Paperback)
ISBN 978-1-64300-582-9 (Digital)

Covenant Books, Inc.
11661 Hwy 707
Murrells Inlet, SC 29576
www.covenantbooks.com

For Jermaine, Alana, and Taylor with love. May your courage lead you to discover your mission in life despite all odds!

Even Before Mia entered school, numbers floated in her head.

Numbers jumped out all around her, in the kitchen, in the car, even while lying in bed.

Her mom worried, "Mia doesn't do what other kids do."

Dad wondered, "Doesn't she play with her blocks and make imaginary stew?"

"Yes," she sighed, "but in the most unusual way."

Let's watch her closely and take notice of patterns while she plays.

Mia sat alone as she always did, carefully cutting Play-Doh and measuring each strip.

The size of each part was the exact same, and she did it in whip!

She counted out numbers, made lines, and dots to mark her place.

She connected her points to make angles and all sorts of shapes.

From room to room, Mia would go,

Calculating, counting, and figuring out all there is to know.

How come the numbers go up to twelve on my ruler and the clock?

Mia counted every line around the combination lock.

In the car she asked, "What is that? Why does it go around and end with an O?

Mom said, "That's an odometer and the numbers ends in zero. The proper names of things you have to know."

Odometer and zero she repeated several times…

Why does each of those zeros have different numbers in front, was the question on her mind?

20, 30, 40, 50 miles per hour, Mia and her mom counted each number as the car went faster and faster…Oh, so fast!

They counted the numbers backwards, and the car slowed down at last.

Dad blurted out, "Maybe she is a little unique."

Mom sighed, "Is it normal for kids to count and calculate every time they speak?

Maybe Mr. Rogers could help us figure this out?

Surely Mia's teacher would help clear up our doubts.

Mr. Rogers paused and said calmly, "Mia's curiosity of calculations and numbers lead me to believe…that Mia is on a mission to be a great mathematician!"

They both exclaimed, "A mathema—who?"

He continued, "Mia counts backwards, forwards, and recognizing all of her numbers. She calculates, solves problems, crunches numbers of all kinds…She has a true mathematician's mind."

Mia sometimes even counts mentally in her head.

She figures out solutions but chooses not to share her answers instead.

Mr. Rogers cleared his voice, "But there is something that concerns me. She sits alone and speaks to no one. I'm beginning to feel Mia is a bit lonely."

So her parents did what any good parents would do.

They set up a play date for her and Ally Lou.

When Ally came to play, she bought her dolls, nail-polish kit, and tea set to display.

"Let's have a tea party first!" she said with smile on her face.

Mia stacked all the tea cups and counted them each.

She grouped them and sorted them by color, size, and put them out of Ally's reach.

12

At lunch, Mia measured the sandwiches into equal parts and shared to make it fair.

She whispered, "I ate four out of four. Do you have any pieces left to spare?

Ally Lou asked, "May I have a cup of water?" Her voice sounded so nice.

Mia used a measuring cup to be precise.

Ally Lou said, "I don't want to play with you."
Mia hung her head low and felt so blue.

Mia's parents watched in amazement. Then it finally hit them. "Mia you have a gift the way that you can calculate and crunch numbers of all sizes. You are on a mission to be a great mathematician!"

That night, they cheered her up by reading math books about flying numbers, books about millions of stripes on a single giraffe, and a book about *100 ways to make 100!*

Mia dreamt that night that she was surrounded by flying numbers while lying in her bed.

She woke up and said, "Being a mathematician is in my head!"

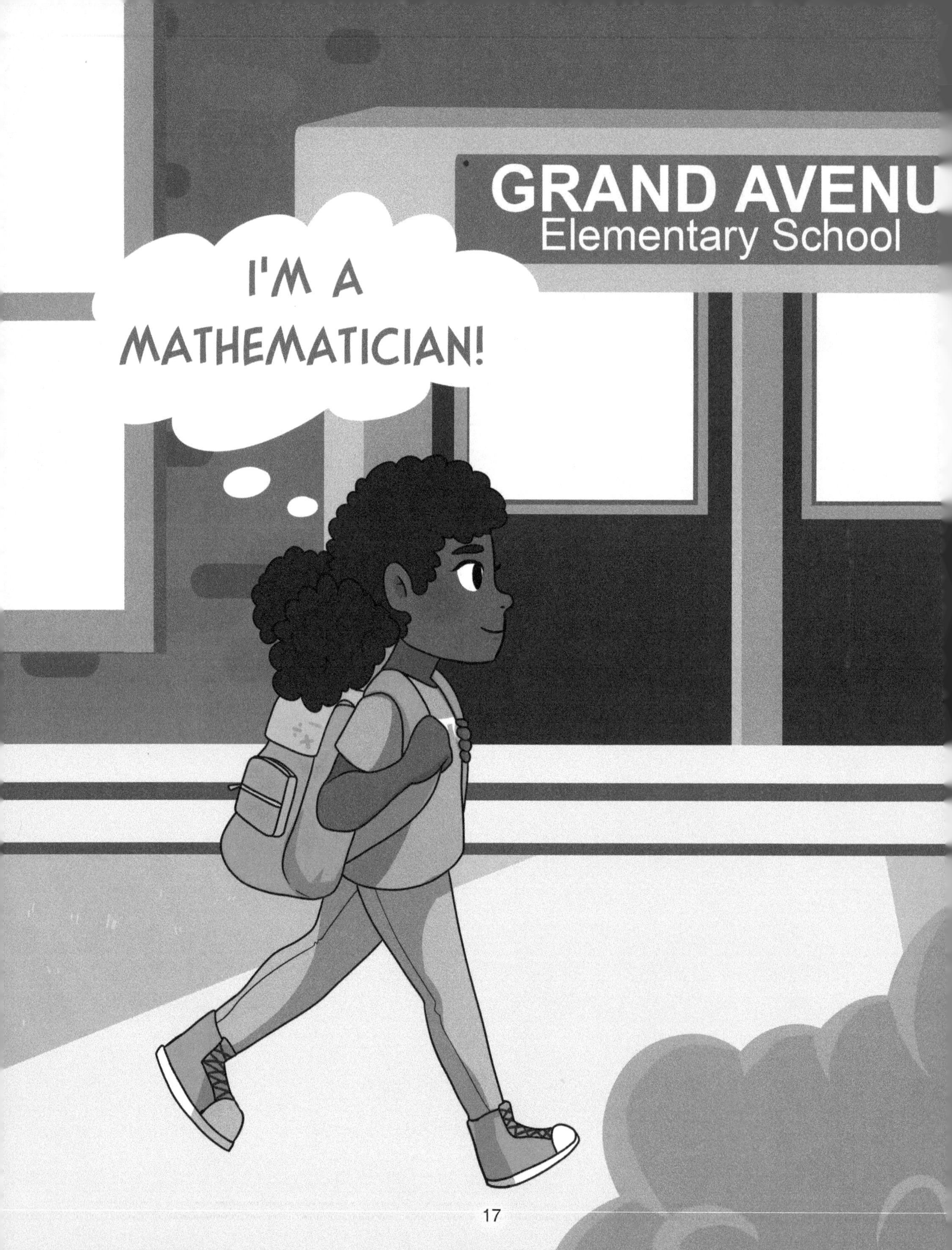
GRAND AVENU
Elementary School
I'M A MATHEMATICIAN!

When she went to school, Mr. Rogers had a word problem on the chart paper for the class to solve; some of the numbers were big, and some were small.

Every one sat quietly when the teacher asked, "How many in all?"

Mia wanted to speak, but she sat quiet and remembered the time her classmates called her a freak.

Then the numbers filled her head, and she said to herself, "A mathematician would not be afraid!" She chose instead to be brave.

Mia began to use mental strategies to comprehend…

"The answer is less than the original number because some were taken away and split among friends…then a friend added on at the end."

She started to mark up her paper then ran out of room and started to mark up her desk right in her classroom!

Then she pushed up her glasses and walked slowly to the chart watching her calculate was a true work of art!

She drew two tens frames and wrote a number sentence underneath.

She drew base ten drawings then crossed out a few. Her classmates sat in disbelief.

Mia did not realize her whole class stood around her and were stunned.

The silence was broken by the sound of Mia's squeaky voice, "One ten and seven ones equals seventeen. All done."

Mr. Rogers smiled, "Quite sophisticated, I'll say!"

Mia you are a mathematician on this very day!

The class jumped up and down to celebrate this quiet kid that they had only just now come to understand. "Mia the mathematician!" They yelled and waved their hands.

Soon Mia's play dates and classroom were filled with mathematicians. One by one, they began to join Mia's mission.

As for Mia, numbers continued to float in her head. Calculating and crunching numbers is what she did.

She continued to learn all that she could…discovering new numbers, patterns, and ways to problem solve…for she was on a mission. Mia the *mathematician!*

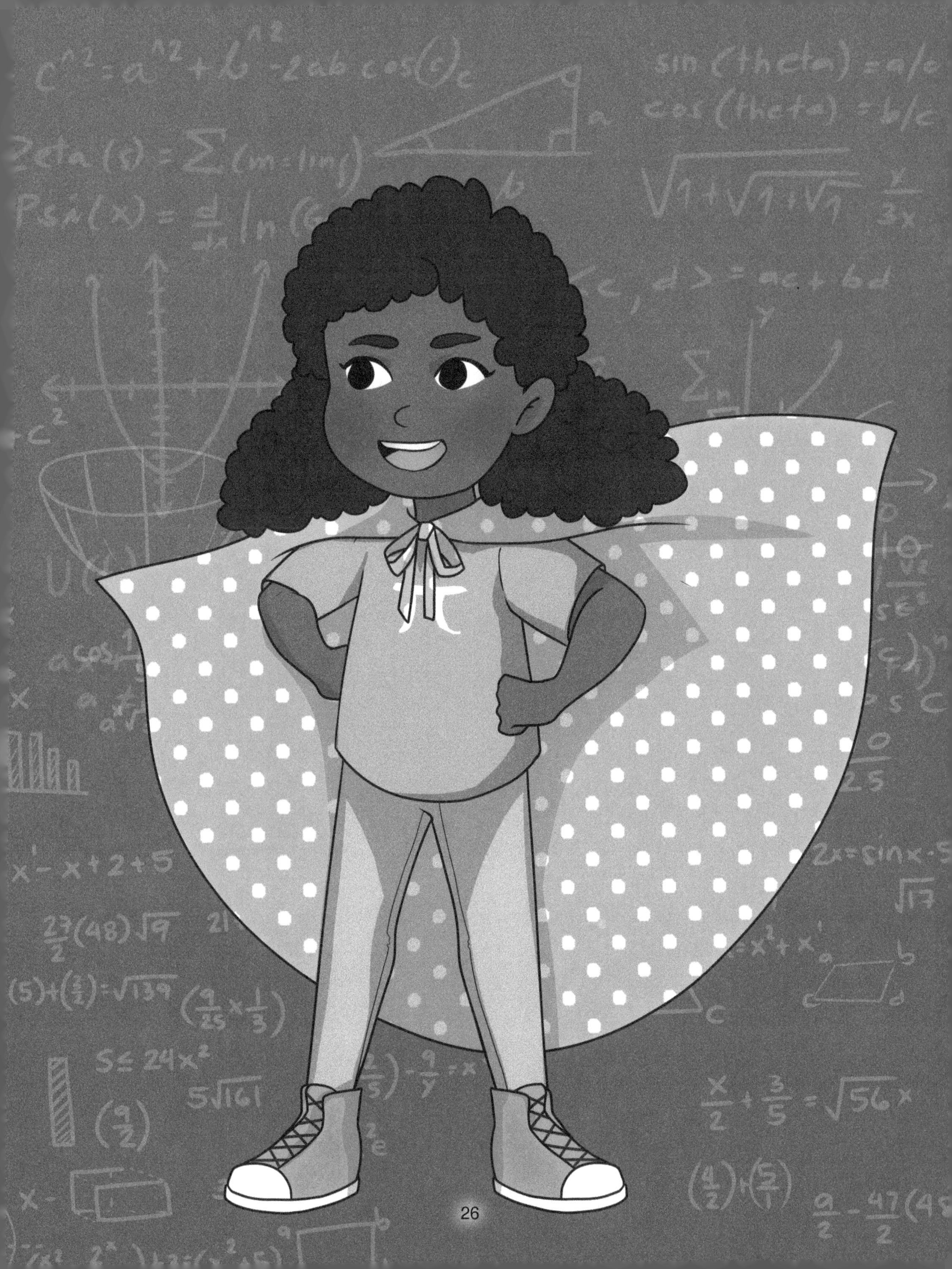

About the Author

Lisa Howerton Goodson spent many years in the education system as a New York City educator and a principal. She is passionate about reading and learning. She loves to spend time with her three children traveling and singing karaoke. She also spends time with her dog Chloe, who by the way, she is still trying to potty train; Not an easy quest! Lisa spends much of her time brainstorming characters and creating stories for children to read. Sometimes even at work, she catches herself brainstorming fascinating characters and stories! She is on a mission just like her newest character Mia! Lisa's mission is to expand the boundaries of children's imagination. Sharing her gift of writing is her purpose and true calling. She lives in Long Island, New York where most days you can find her curled up reading a good book or somewhere (couch, deck, airport, mall) doing what she loves best—writing!

CPSIA information can be obtained
at www.ICGtesting.com
Printed in the USA
LVHW071748010719
622877LV00009B/32/P

9 781643 005812